Nat, Nat, the Nantucket Cat Goes to the Beach

Written by **Peter W. Barnes and Cheryl Shaw Barnes**

Illustrated by **Susan Arciero**

Other books by Peter and Cheryl Barnes

Woodrow, the White House Mouse, about the presidency and the nation's most famous mansion.

Woodrow For President, about how Woodrow got to the White House.

House Mouse, Senate Mouse, about Congress and the legislative process.

Marshall, the Courthouse Mouse, about the Supreme Court and the judicial process.

A "Mice" Way to Learn About Government teachers curriculum guide.

A "Mice" Way to Learn about Voting, Campaigns and Elections teachers curriculum guide, for *Woodrow for President.*

Capital Cooking with Woodrow and Friends, a cookbook for kids that mixes fun recipes with fun facts about American history and government.

Alexander, the Old Town Mouse, about historic Old Town, Alexandria, Va., across the Potomac River from Washington, D.C.

Nat, Nat, the Nantucket Cat, (with Susan Arciero) about beautiful Nantucket Island, Mass.

Martha's Vineyard, about wonderful Martha's Vineyard, Mass.

Cornelius Vandermouse, the Pride of Newport, about historic Newport, R.I., home to America's most magnificent mansion houses.

Order these books through your local bookstore by title, or order **autographed copies** of the Barnes' books by calling 1-800-441-1949, or from our website at **www.VSPBooks.com.**

For a brochure and ordering information, write to:

VSP Books
P.O. Box 17011
Alexandria, VA 22302

To get on our mailing list, send your name and address to the address above.

Copyright © 2001 by Peter W. Barnes and Cheryl Shaw Barnes

ISBN   1-893622-05-3

Library of Congress Catalog Card Number: 2001 135156

10 9 8 7 6 5 4 3 2

Printed in the United States of America

This book is dedicated to
Curtis and Joan Barnes, our parents,
who have brought joy to our families
by sharing their island with us.

—P.W.B and C.S.B.

For Emerson and your beach days on Nantucket.

—S.A.

Nat, Nat, the Nantucket Cat, walked one sunny day
Down a nice Nantucket street, his own Nantucket way.
"What a very pretty morning," he purred so happily.
"A pretty morning on our pretty island in the sea."

On special days like this, he thought, there's just one thing to do!
Grab your towel and sunglasses, and call a friend or two,
And meet them on your favorite beach in wonderful Nantucket—
And don't forget the sun tan cream, your shovel and your bucket!

Down the street on cobblestones ran Nat, the happy cat,
To find his best Nantucket friend, the famous Captain Pat,

Past the public library (it's called the "Atheneum"),
Down the lane and to the left, behind the old museum.

A little cottage on the lane is home to Captain Pat.
He's napping in his hammock there, his head beneath his hat.
"How can you sleep on such a day?!?" a frisky Nat meowed.
(To make sure Pat was waking up, he meowed rather loud!)

"Who is that?" said Captain Pat, rubbing both his eyes.
"Why Nat, my furry, purry friend—I'm pleasantly surprised!"
"We're going to the beach," Nat said. "Now get your towel and bike!
You can drive and I will give directions, if you like!"

They rode past many cottages behind the picket fences,
With trellises of roses high that tickled all the senses.
And when the smell of sea and salt was heavy in the air,
And when the sand came into sight, they knew that they were there!

They parked the bike and grabbed their things and headed for the ocean,
With towels and hats and chairs and books—a regular commotion!
And cats, you know, are very, very sensitive to sun;
So they brought the kitty sun block, SPF of 91!

"This looks good!" said Captain Pat, who juggled all their stuff.
"No," said Nat, "Move over there—this isn't close enough!"
But soon they had a cozy spot, their blanket on the beach,
The ocean waves before them and their soda at their reach.

As the sun rose higher in the blue Nantucket sky,
Others came to spend the day and found their spots nearby.

Mommies with their babies sweet and sisters with their brothers,
Daddies, Grandmas, Grandpas, too, and many, many, others.

Now its time to take a dip in old Nantucket Sound.
(The locals say it really is the swellest swim around!)

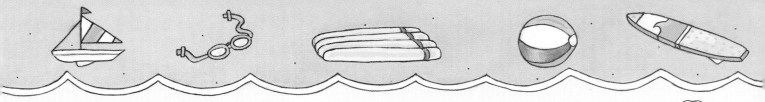

Catch a wave and dive and splash! Come Nat! Come everyone!
But cats and water—well, you know. He'd rather *watch* the fun.

Later, there's a contest to build castles made of sand.
Captain Pat went right to work and built one rather grand.
So did many children—so did a certain cat.
The winner, said the judges, was, of course, our good friend Nat!

Take a walk along the beach to find a stone or shell—
There's a scallop, there's a clam—sometimes it's hard to tell.
A hermit crab goes walking by, a fascinating creature—
Look for other things here with your parents or your teacher.

moon snail
shell

ark shell

horseshoe
crab

Atlantic surf
clam shell

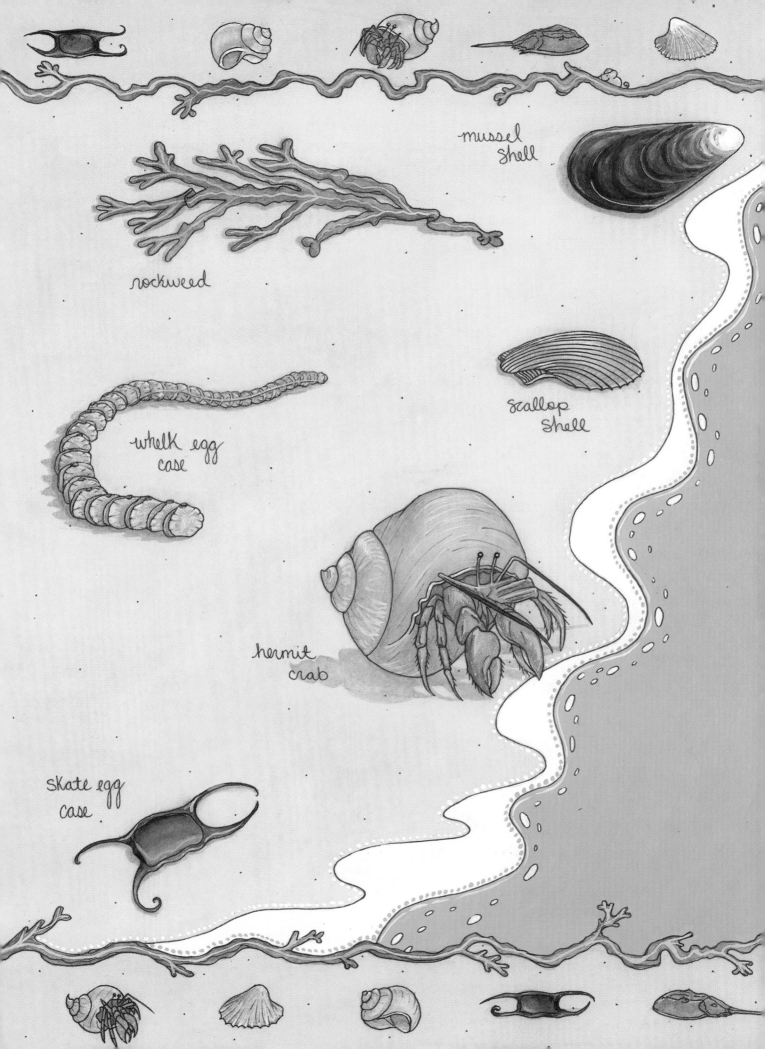

mussel
Shell

rockweed

scallop
Shell

whelk egg
case

hermit
crab

Skate egg
case

Nat and Captain Pat agree it's time for something cold—
Let's go to the snack stand, then, where ice cream cones are sold!
Captain Pat gets chocolate chip, but see how Nat's eye twinkles
When he gets a double cherry, topped with catnip sprinkles!

Time to toss the Frisbee for a bit of exercise—
Run and jump and laugh beneath the blue Nantucket skies.
Nat likes chasing Frisbees rolling high or underneath—
He throws them with his tail and he can catch them in his teeth!

Now the sun begins to set along the distant water—
What a day, but time for every parent, son and daughter,
For Captains and their kitty cats, to leave the ocean's splash—
Pack your towels and books and toys—and please pick up your trash!

Captain Pat climbs on his bike
    and pedals soft and slow—
He looks down in the basket
    on the handlebars below:
Nat lies sleeping, long before
    the Captain's house they reach,
Dreaming of his special day
    on his Nantucket beach…

Nantucket Beaches

There are many beautiful beaches in Nantucket, Here are some of the most popular:

Children's Beach, located in the harbor, sheltered in town. A good place for small children, with events sponsored in the summer season by the Nantucket Park and Recreation Commission. There is a park with a playground.

Jetties Beach, located just outside town and named for the rock pile jetty that stretches out from the beach into Nantucket sound. Families like it because of its proximity to restrooms, recreation rentals, tennis courts and a snack bar. It is accessible from town by bike or shuttle bus. There is plenty of parking for those who drive.

Steps Beach, named for the long steps that a visitor must descend to reach the beach, The steps begin at the end of path at the corner of Lincoln Circle, off of Cliff Road. It is more private than Jetties Beach and has a gentle surf. .

Dionis Beach, popular among locals and visitors for its isolation and lack of crowds. Three miles from town by bike or vehicle. Dunes shelter the beach and the water is usually calm for swimming.

Cisco, a popular out-of-town beach at the end of Hummock Pond Road, four miles by bike or car. It has fewer crowds and heavy surf.

Madaket Beach, located on the far west side of the island, five miles from town by bus or bike. Famous for its sunsets.

Miacomet, a beach with strong surf—be careful. But nearby is **Miacomet Pond**. Its lack of surf and currents make it safer for young children.

Nobadeer, popular among teenagers and college-age visitors to the island. Located near the airport, it is great place to watch to planes land and depart.

Surfside, at the end of Surfside Road, a three-mile bike ride on a paved path. It is also accessible by car or bus. It has a wide beach, which makes it popular for picnics and beach games.

Siasconset, in the quiet village of 'Sconset, a seven-mile bike, car or bus ride from town.

Write Here About
Your Nantucket Adventure